This book lives on the shelf of

....

A Pardalote Press publication, 2023
ISBN 978-0-6455634-2-9

www.pardalotepress.com
Printed in Australia by SOS Print+Media, Sydney

A catalogue record for this book is available from the National Library of Australi

Secrets of the Good Fairy House

Sophie Masson

Lorena Carrington

Introduction

Secrets of the Good Fairy House is an imaginative exploration of how a beloved childhood house can grant not only a treasury of rich memories, but also help to spark creative inspiration. For both Lorena and I, there is such a house. They were on opposite sides of the world. Mine was a centuries-old house set in a sleepy little village in south-west France; Lorena's a post-war house in a bustling regional town in Victoria. But though separated by distance, time and culture, each was and continues to be a good-fairy house for us as creators. For the good fairy house isn't just bricks and mortar and furnishings; it certainly isn't just real estate, or a mere address. And whether or not that good fairy house is still in the family—mine isn't, Lorena's is—her gifts of memory and enchantment endure to this day. For our good-fairy houses helped to weave the magic that would one day turn dreamy children into creators: myself a writer, Lorena an artist.

This book is not straight-out memoir or straight-out fiction; it is a mix of both. In words and images, we've interwoven bits from both houses and bits from imagined places, to create something new, a unique recreation of the secrets of the good fairy house.

We hope you enjoy exploring the good fairy house, and invite you to go on a journey into the secrets of your own special house.

Sophie Masson

Open the door and come in

It was the biggest key the child had ever seen. It looked like the key to a castle in a fairy tale. And the knocker was like something in a fairy tale too. A slightly creepy one, because it was a lady's ringed hand, holding a ball. You couldn't see the rest of the person that hand belonged to. Unless you glanced quickly out of the corner of your eye—and there she was, with a twinkle in her eye and a finger to her lips. And then the child knew: this was not a scary place, this was not Bluebeard's castle. This was the good-fairy house and magic would happen here.

One day, long into the future, the child's children would grow up, on the other side of the world, in a good-fairy house of their own. The knocker on that door would be a beringed hand, holding a ball. And if you glanced quickly, out of the corner of your eye, you might see someone, with a twinkle in her eye and a finger to her lips...

Light

Day: Look! There are magical beasts taking shape in the wavering dancing light falling in layers from the coloured glass of the door. Hold out a hand to touch them...and oh, they're gone. But ah, then they're back, and they're new, they've changed...

Night: Look! As I stand at the door of our house, there are tall golden flowers of light wherever I look. The town is blooming with light, the gold dancing across the darkness, rivalling the silver stars high above. Hold out a hand to it and it's outlined with light, as if you have got magic spreading out from your fingertips...

Hall clock

The hall is quiet. Except for the clock. The clock is not silent. It goes tick-tock. And bong bong BONG! The clock has a name. It's called Gerard. But Grandfather too, and that's not the same! It has a window. It has a door. Like a little house. Too small for us. But just right for a mouse.

Hickory dickory dock! The mouse ran up the clock...My brother screams, my sister laughs. Hickory dickory dock!

One day an old, old man came to the door of our good-fairy house. He used to live there. He saw our clock. He said, When I was small a man came to our door. With a bear! A real bear! And I was so frightened I hid in our clock.

Wow, we thought. Maybe he'd turned into a mouse?

A study in transformations

Come into the study. It has windows onto the quiet street. A big writing desk, a comfy chair. An old Persian carpet. And books. Some in shelves, some in a tall bookcase with filigreed doors, like a kind of grille. It has a private look, like the grille in a convent, or a confessional. But open the doors, and you can see that the books look cosily at home. Near the bookcase is the neat desk, with its chessboard top made of squares of wood, some golden, some chestnut-coloured. On it sit a lamp, a leather pad so you won't scratch the desk when you're writing, an inkstand just for decoration because biros are what's used now.

But that private bookcase and that neat desk have a secret. A big secret! Two were once one. One oak barrel. Yes, a barrel for wine! An old oak barrel found lonely and shabby in a shed, when the family first bought the good-fairy house. Then a magic wand was waved over it, woodwork elves set to work—and hey presto! Transformation. One became two, barrel became bookcase and desk, no more fermentation, but instead reading. And writing. Only—wait--those are fermentations too, right? Words, thoughts, stories, ideas: the old oak barrel now steeped in a different kind of intoxicating mix.

Talking plates

What story can you tell us today, plates, as we sit at the table? No talking from us, it's not allowed, but they won't hear you if you speak.

I can tell you a story about hunting. I can tell you a story about cakes. I can tell you a story that will make you laugh. I can tell you a story that will make you cry. I can tell you about a saint. I can tell you about a dancer. I can tell you any story you want to hear.

And I can tell you a secret...

Chest of drawers

Open a drawer. And there are treasures. Secret notebooks, with stories and pictures and things pasted in. A mirror. Old pictures. A dagger. A feather. It's brown. It belongs to an owl. The owl who lives in the old elm tree and hoots at night. It's a lonely sound. And look, leaves dotted with codes, clues, spy messages: the wind blew them from the wild in at the door, one day. Or was it really the wind? I run my fingers over the leaves and feel, through my skin, the whisper of secrets...

CHRISTOPHER JOHNSON & Co's
CELEBRATED
ELECTRO PLATE
WESTERN WORKS
SHEFFIELD.
MADE IN ENGLAND
Warranted British Manufacture
TAYLOR'S
CELEBRATED
WITNESS
TABLE CUTLERY
MADE BY NEEDHAM, VEALL AND TYZACK LTD
AT EYE WITNESS WORKS, SHEFFIELD, ENGLAND.
STAINLESS
MADE IN ENGLAND.
TAYLOR'S
CELEBRATED
WITNESS
TABLE CUTLERY
NEEDHAM, VEALL & TYZACK LTD
SHEFFIELD
1946
To my Darling
With happy thoughts on your birthday and with all my love.
John
xxx

Wardrobe

You can climb in. It's big. Very big. For hide and seek, it's great. You can slip behind the long old fur coats, stay quiet as a mouse, and maybe they won't find you. Or maybe—maybe you will put out a hand to the back of the wardrobe and there won't be a back anymore, there'll be snowflakes landing on your hand instead. And you'll see a light shining on a path beyond. It's happened! It's really happened!

You'll put on a coat. You'll step out into the snow. And then—well, you hope they won't find you: the Witch, the wolf, the dwarf.

Photographs

So many stories, so many secrets, in the faces smiling from their frames in the good-fairy house...Golden glamour and broken hearts, glittering balls and beachy fashion, children's toys and feathery hats—so much to see, and wonder, and imagine, about this enchanted world of vanished moments and long-ago drama. But the good-fairy house whispers, still it continues, not vanished, just sleeping, in your veins, and your bones, and your dreams...

Many Happy
of the day. Dear
All my Love.
From New Guinea.
Jack

Pictures

Pictures on the walls, pictures in books.

Some are just pictures. They sit there waiting for you to look.

Others—well, they are not the waiting kind. They catch you by surprise, they take you on a wild ride into another world. Which ones are they? Hush—that's a secret!

A DREAM OF YOUNG SUMMER
From Harper's Magazine.

Magic carpet

The floor is no longer just the floor. It has become a landing pad. The carpet is no longer just a beautiful thing to cover creaking boards. It has become a sky-sailor, taking us into lands far away and long ago...

Patterns and threads

Memories are spun on the wheel of time—careful not to prick your finger!--moments are woven through our minds, patterning our lives in crisscrossing threads. Sometimes a thread will snag and then a pattern of memory changes, transforms, turns into a new pattern, a new way of looking into the past...

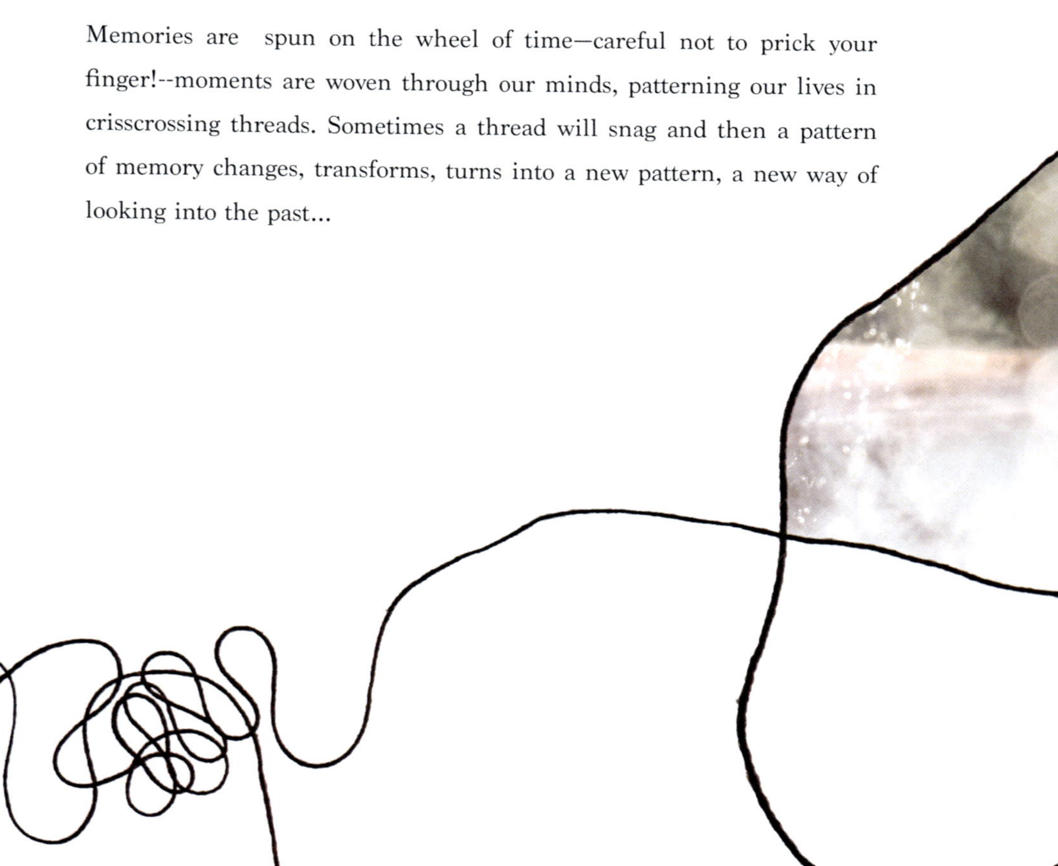

Miniature world

I think one day I'll catch them at it—the miniature people in their miniature world, the tiny planet spinning in the universe of our house. If I stay awake long enough, if I open my eyes early enough, I'll see them move from their shelves and their nooks and their cabinets behind glass. They'll be having a party. They'll be playing music. They'll be chatting, twirling parasols and fans, chasing butterflies, fishing, playing cards, falling in love.... Until they see me—then they freeze. They pretend they never moved. They pretend they sit there all day all night and never move. But I know better. And one day, I'll catch them at it!

Ghosts and echoes

The house holds sad secrets, as well as happy ones. Echoes of sorrow as well as joy. In one room, the sunniest room, oh so beautiful it was, it is said that a young man perished for love, once, a long time ago...and sometimes on dark nights, you could sense his presence. Not angry, not dangerous—but sad, sad beyond bearing. But the sun shines still in that room and that is not a contradiction. Though it seemed to me to be that at the time. A haunted room should be creepy, not beautiful. A haunted room should be dark and shadowy not golden and glorious with sun...So I was not afraid. And perhaps that was also a gift of the good-fairy house.

Garden

Out from the French windows, onto the terrace, down the stone steps into the world of our garden. Only our garden is so big we call it the park. Long ago, a great king held court under our giant old elm tree, only it wasn't old then, it was young... An owl lives in its branches and at night we hear it hoot, and sometimes a fox prowls around its roots looking for mice. A fox can scream and that sends a shiver up your spine, like the hoot of the owl. In spring we sit in the cherry tree stuffing ourselves and in autumn we do the same with the figs and the greengages, juice running down our chins and tummies fit to burst... We play at tigers in ambush and make daisy crowns with violets as jewels and we look for ladybirds and dragonflies and delicate empty birds' eggs that have fallen from nests. We roam everywhere, in our garden that is also a park, except for two places: the swampy ground at

the very back where the thick, patterned poisonous snakes called vipers lurk, ready to dash out like lightning, and the closed up old well where it's said once a wicked witch was flung. But once we were passing by the well and saw a huge old toad sitting on the cover of the well, looking at us with yellow eyes, and we thought that maybe the witch had got out, so we RAN!

There's a story I read in one of my books where a fairy puts a spell on two sisters: whenever the kind one speaks, roses, pearls and diamonds come out of her mouth and when the cruel sister speaks, toads and snakes come out of hers. Imagine that! No-one wants to be spewing up toads and snakes of course but diamonds and pearls might choke you too, maybe that's not the cleverest good-fairy spell ever, I thought...

Dreams in the good fairy house

Everything is quiet. Everyone is in their beds. Sleep comes. Dreams come. What will we see tonight? Who will we meet?

A bad dream comes... The hallway curves and winds like a path. There's a big fish tank, two monsters behind it, their size distorted by the water. One steps out. It's huge and blue and furry! It chases the child into the kitchen from the other side of the house, where she lies across a chair and screams herself awake. She draws that dream more than once, the looming tall monster, the quivering smudgy shape on the chair...

A good dream comes...the bedroom door has turned into a green archway and through it the child can see trees with leaves of silver and gold and crystal, making tinkling sounds like bells. She can hear music as she steps through the green and in the distance she can see girls dancing, they look like the girls on the wallpaper of her room. She picks a leaf from a tree and holds it in her hand...and suddenly she wakes. And on the floor she sees the book that had fallen from the bed, The Twelve Dancing Princesses. On it is a dead leaf! Or did she dream that too? She's not sure, any more...

The house remembers

Everything is quiet. Everyone is asleep. But the house stirs. The house wakes. The house remembers...

The houses that inspired us

Sophie

The very year I was born, my parents, who were then working as expatriates in Indonesia, bought their first house, with the help of my paternal grandmother and great-grandmother, who'd scouted out properties for them. The house was a large, beautiful but crumbling late-eighteenth/early nineteenth century house, with dilapidated seventeenth century outbuildings, in a south-western French village called Empeaux. It was an unfashionable, eccentric and cheap buy at the time—for back then Empeaux was thought to be much too remote from the city—mon Dieu, a whole thirty-five kilometres from Toulouse!-- for most people to want to live there. Besides, the house had been allowed to go to rack and ruin, and there was heaps of work to do in it and in the large overgrown parklands that surrounded it, with its ancient trees. Much too much, most people thought.

Well, nothing daunted, my parents set to work or rather set their expatriate salaries to work, first in Indonesia and then in Australia, paying a succession of masons, tilers, electricians, roofers, painters, carpenters, gardeners and lots more local tradesmen, who slowly but surely, under my parents' guiding hand, turned neglected Cinderella into a beautiful princess admired by all. And as we settled into a routine of three years in Australia, three months in France, the house became our French base.

It was an utterly magical place. A house my parents were happy in and relaxed, and from where we children could roam into the countryside, free of the anxious parental worrying which in Australia tethered us to our immediate surroundings. It was holiday, it was enchantment, it was adventure, it was the other world, where anything was possible. Back in Australia, we lived a rather restricted life, enclosed in a French world at home, an Australian one at school, with each not meeting, only parallel. Folded in on the nucleus of family, we had to devise most of our own entertainments. Back in Australia, I would tell stories of fairies and knights and monsters to my siblings, huddling under a table covered with a velvet curtain so I could conjure up an atmosphere of darkness and mystery. But in our good fairy house and the French rural world beyond it, we discovered the actual homes of those fairies and knights and monsters—and ghosts!

Our good-fairy house nurtured people, especially children, and all of us very much grown-up children remember it with huge fondness and a real melancholy. For it is lost to us now—in the early 90's, after they'd returned permanently to France, my parents sold the house and moved to another region. But it is not lost in our memory: every bit of it still vivid in our minds and hearts. I can still walk the corridors and stairs and go into each room, in my memory. And I still go and visit it when I am back in France, as do my siblings. We can't go inside, but we can stand there, and remember. For it is a house that haunts anyone who's ever lived in it—even when we were living there, former residents would sometimes drop by to look at it again just like we do now--a house that forever becomes a part of your emotional and imaginative DNA. 'Elle a une âme,' my mother said to me once, referring to the house, 'it has a soul. It's the only house we've lived in that appears in my dreams.' That means even more to me now, for Maman as well as Mamizou, Betty and Geneviève, our grandmother and aunts on Dad's side, are buried in the quiet village churchyard, only a few steps away from the house....

Lorena

My good-fairy house has been in the family for several generations, and seems to keep being passed down the maternal line. I grew up there, as did my mother. Her mother built the house with my grandfather in 1946, but grew up in the house that was there before. When they were little, my daughters played there with my old toys, read my mum's old books, and tried on my grandmother's dresses, and we ate lunch in the side of the house that was built for my great grandmother, so she could live there with her daughter and granddaughters. One of those granddaughters, my mother, lives there now. It's a puzzle that fits together through some inextricable logic, evidenced by cupboards of wedding china, generations of dolls, and many collected treasures.

There might not be ghosts, but a house can be haunted by many things; love, the layers of memories from so many lives entwined.

Memory Maps

Downstairs

Dad's study / library

Front door

Hall

Small dining room

Large dining room

Large Salon

Stairs

Antechamber - storage + exploring

Kitchen

Hall

French doors leading to big terrace + huge garden full of fruit trees

Pantry (in walls)

Toilet

Laundry

Upstairs

Stairs to attics (creepy! 2 rooms)

Antechamber - storage + exploring

Red room (sunny but haunted)

Corridor

Brown room (sunny + not haunted!)

Antechamber - storage + exploring!

Green room (outside the window a big elm tree, where an owl lived)

Stairs to downstairs

Blue room (huge wardrobe where we played Narnia; weird vibe in room)

Outside

Big medieval outbuildings in mud-brick, ~~barns, garage~~, loft

Sophie's childhood home

Memory maps are simple things, yet powerful things. You don't need to be a cartographer or an artist to create a memory map. They can be as rough as you like or as elaborate as you like. And they are a brilliant way to spark off memories and stories of your own good-fairy house!

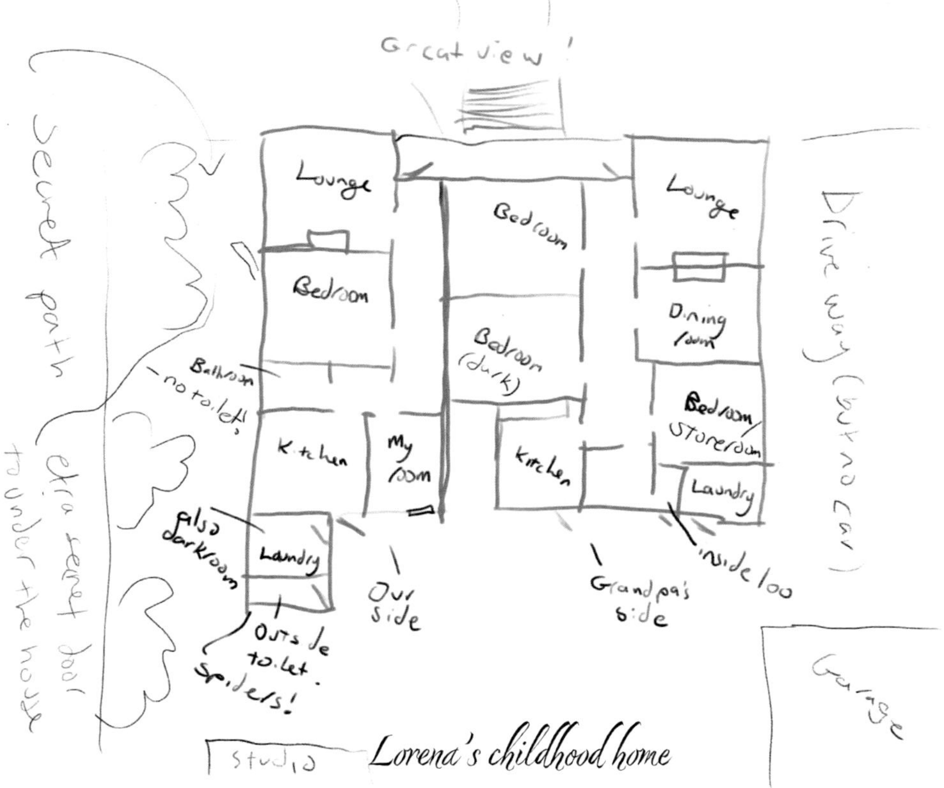

Lorena's childhood home

Activities

Here are some activities to explore your own (real or imagined) good fairy house:

*Create a memory map, choose one of the rooms or spaces to focus on, and write down or draw your impressions/memories of it. You can also extend that by choosing an object from that room/space and creating a short text about it.

*Imagine you are the 'good fairy' of the house, remembering your people: write impressions of them over time. Or draw them: think about the clothes they might have worn, and their day-to-day activities. How are they different and similar to now?

*On a practical level: consider doing some research to extend your own experience/observations of the house, for example, finding information on when the house was built and by who. You might find material from family, friends, and neighbours as well as local councils, history groups and newspapers, and State archives(online). You can also check out the National Library's helpful checklist for house research, https://www.nla.gov.au/faq/how-do-i-trace-the-history-of-my-house

Houses can feel like a maze sometimes. Can you take the key to unlock the house in the middle? Eagle eyes might have noticed that this maze is based on the memory map of Lorena's childhood home.

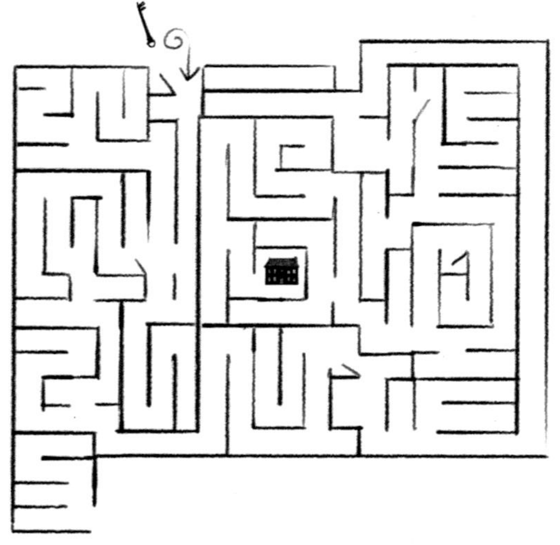